THUDD

Hiya! My name Thudd. Best robot friend of Drewd. Thudd know lots of stuff. How stars get born. Where planets come from. What happened to dinosaurs.

Drewd and Unkie Al like to invent stuff. Unkie invent time machine. Oop! Drewd have snack accident. Drewd and Oody go back in time! Want to come? Turn page, please!

Get lost with
Andrew, Judy, and Thudd
in all their exciting adventures!

Andrew Lost on the Dog
Andrew Lost in the Bathroom
Andrew Lost in the Kitchen
Andrew Lost in the Garden
Andrew Lost Under Water
Andrew Lost in the Whale
Andrew Lost on the Reef
Andrew Lost in the Deep
Andrew Lost in Time
Andrew Lost on Earth

AND COMING SOON!
Andrew Lost with the Dinosaurs

ANDREW LOST

10

ON EARTH

BY J. C. GREENBURG

ILLUSTRATED
BY JAN GERARDI

A STEPPING STONE BOOK™

Random House 🏠 New York

To Dan, Zack, and the real Andrew,
with a galaxy of love.
To the children who read these books: I wish
you wonderful questions. Questions are
telescopes into the universe!
—J.C.G.

To Cathy Goldsmith, with many thanks.
—J.G.

www.randomhouse.com/kids/AndrewLost
www.AndrewLost.com

Library of Congress Cataloging-in-Publication Data
Greenburg, J. C. (Judith C.)
On earth / by J. C. Greenburg ; illustrated by Jan Gerardi. — 1st ed.
  p.   cm. — (Andrew lost ; 10)   A Stepping Stone book.
SUMMARY: While bouncing through Earth's prehistory in a
malfunctioning time machine, Andrew, his cousin Judy, and Thudd
the robot meet Doctor Kron-Tox's nephew, Beeper, and nearly lose
the Time-A-Tron in a tsunami.
ISBN 0-375-82950-4 (trade) — ISBN 0-375-92950-9 (lib. bdg.)
[1. Time travel—Fiction. 2. Inventions—Fiction.
3. Cousins—Fiction. 4. Earth—History.] I. Gerardi, Jan, ill.
II. Title. III. Series: Greenburg, J. C. (Judith C.). Andrew lost ; v 10.
PZ7.G82785 Ol 2005   [Fic]—dc22   2004009281

Printed in the United States of America
First Edition 10 9 8

CONTENTS

ANDREW'S WORLD

Andrew Dubble

Andrew is ten years old, but he's been inventing things since he was four. Andrew's inventions usually get him into trouble, like the time he shrunk himself, his cousin Judy, and his little silver robot Thudd smaller than a mosquito's toe with the Atom Sucker.

Today a problem with a snack has sent Andrew traveling through time—to the beginning of planet Earth!

Judy Dubble

Judy is Andrew's thirteen-year-old cousin. At nine o'clock, she got into her pajamas in a cabin in Montana. A few minutes later, there wasn't a cabin, there wasn't a Montana . . . there wasn't even an *Earth*! According to Judy, it's all Andrew's fault.

Thudd

The **Handy Ultra-Digital Detective**. Thudd is a super-smart robot and Andrew's best friend. He has helped to save Andrew and Judy from deadly octopuses, killer jellyfish, and the giant squid. But can he save them from an asteroid the size of the planet Mars?

Uncle Al

Andrew and Judy's uncle is a top-secret scientist. He invented Thudd and the Time-A-Tron time-travel machine. But before he finished the Time-A-Tron, he

2

was kidnapped and hidden in one of Earth's ice ages! Will Andrew and Judy be able to find him?

The Time-A-Tron

It looks like a giant cooking timer, but it's really a time-travel machine. Too bad Uncle Al got kidnapped before he could make sure it worked!

Doctor Kron-Tox

The mysterious Doctor Kron-Tox invented a time machine, too—the Tick-Tox Box. He's used it to kidnap Uncle Al and another scientist. But why?

Beeper Jones

Say hello to Doctor Kron-Tox's nephew. He likes to collect monster cockroaches and gigunda centipedes. Other than that, he's not a bad kid!

BURIED ALIVE!

KRAAAAAAAAK-UKK-UKKK-UKKKK!

"Holy moly!" hollered Andrew Dubble. "It feels like an earthquake!"

Another giant asteroid smashed into the Time-A-Tron time machine. Andrew and his thirteen-year-old cousin Judy bounced in their big blue seat.

Just two hours ago, they'd been pigging out on pizza with their Uncle Al. Now asteroids were burying them inside the very beginning of planet Earth!

In front of Andrew and Judy's chair was a control panel. Its digital display flashed:

4 BILLION 500 MILLION YEARS AGO

Judy looked up through the clear dome of the Time-A-Tron. All she could see was solid rock!

"Cheese Louise!" she grumped. "These stupid asteroids and comets stick together like snowballs! We're trapped inside tons of rock!"

meep . . . "Asteroids and comets make planets," squeaked a voice from Andrew's pajama pocket.

It was Thudd, Andrew's little silver robot and best friend.

bong . . . "That is right, little one," said the Time-A-Tron. "Without asteroids, there would be no solid Earth, no air. Without comets, there would be little water."

"Oh, clap a lid on it, guys!" said Judy. "All I want to know is how to get out of here." She banged the heel of her slipper on the Fast-Forward button.

When it worked, the Fast-Forward button

moved the Time-A-Tron forward through time.

Flack! Flack! Flack!

But there were no balls of green light. The Time-A-Tron's Fast-Fins wouldn't spin.

bong . . . "I am afraid the Fast-Fins are stuck in stone," said the Time-A-Tron. "If the Fast-Fins cannot spin, we cannot move forward in time."

Judy pushed her face close to Andrew's. "This is all your fault, Bug-Brain," she said. "If you hadn't gotten your stupid fudge stuck on the Fast-Back button, we wouldn't have traveled to the beginning of the universe in our pajamas!"

meep . . . "Drewd! Oody! Look!" squeaked Thudd. He was pointing to the Super-Peeper.

The Super-Peeper looked like a pumpkin-sized snow globe. It could show what was happening anywhere in the universe. Right now, it showed a sky full of asteroids . . . speeding toward baby Earth!

KEEERUCCKK! GRAAACK! SPLURSH!

Through the dome of the Time-A-Tron, Andrew watched the rock around them start to glow and melt and swirl.

"Yowzers!" yelled Andrew.

"Yiiiikes!" hollered Judy.

meep . . . "Giant asteroids hit hard, hard, hard!" said Thudd. "Make heat. Clapping hands make little heat. Smashing asteroids make big heat! Rocks melt!"

Thudd pointed to the much bigger Earth that now appeared in the Super-Peeper.

meep . . . "Baby Earth getting born! Getting big!"

Judy rolled her eyes. "I wish the Earth would get born somewhere else," she said.

Suddenly the Time-A-Tron was tumbling along a river of flaming rock.

bong . . . "We are following the molecules of Montana again!" said the Time-A-Tron.

Montana was where they had started. The Time-A-Tron could move through time. But the only way it could move through space was to follow the molecules of Montana.

Andrew squinted up at the dome of the Time-A-Tron. He was looking for cracks and bubbles. "Um, will the Time-A-Tron start to melt like when we were close to the beginning of the universe?" he asked.

bong . . . "The temperature was a billion degrees then, Master Andrew," said the Time-

A-Tron. "This rock soup is only two thousand degrees."

Andrew's eyebrows went up. "Judy, try the Fast-Forward button again," he said. "Now that the rocks are soft, maybe the Fast-Fins can move."

Judy slammed the Fast-Forward button again.

Flack! Flack! Flack!

HNNNN . . . HNNNN . . . WOOHOOOOO!

The Time-A-Tron jiggled. Sparks of bright green light flashed outside the dome.

"Green sparks!" said Andrew. "The Fast-Fins are working!"

BLAFOOOOOOM!

bong . . . "We are off!" said the Time-A-Tron.

BUH-BUH-BUH ZNERKKK!

The green sparks disappeared.

bong . . . "Oh dear!" said the Time-A-Tron. "We've moved only ten thousand years ahead."

They were still in the gushing rock river. It was carrying them toward the surface of baby Earth.

"Look!" said Andrew, pointing to the top of the Time-A-Tron's dome. "I see stars!"

2

SPLURSHHHH!

The Time-A-Tron bobbed to the surface of an ocean of fiery melted rock. Above, the night sky sparkled with stars.

"Cheese Louise!" cried Judy. "Where's the land? Where's the water?"

Andrew peered out through the dome. "This sure is a weird place," he said. "But it's too dark to see much. There isn't even any moonlight."

meep . . . "Earth like this *everywhere*," said Thudd. "Big ball of melted rock."

bong . . . "And there is no moonlight," said the Time-A-Tron, "because there is no moon."

"Sure," said Andrew. "On some nights you can't see the moon at all."

bong . . . "Pardon me, Master Andrew," said the Time-A-Tron. "The moon does not yet *exist*!"

"I bet I know what you're going to say," said Judy. "One of these giant asteroids starts buzzing around the Earth and that's how we get a moon."

"Noop, noop, noop!" said Thudd. "Moon happen different way."

"How?" asked Judy.

meep . . . "Oody not want to know," said Thudd.

"Oh yes, I do," said Judy. "Spit it out, Thudd."

meep . . . "Moon happen when planet big as Mars crash into Earth," said Thudd. "Lotsa stuff splash into space. Make moon!"

Judy shivered. "What if this thing crashes on *us*?"

Out of the corner of his eye, Andrew saw

a flash. A bright ball of light was streaking across the sky.

"I hope that's not the Mars-sized thing!" cried Judy.

"Noop, noop, noop!" said Thudd. "Comet coming now. Big ball of ice!"

Suddenly the purple button in the middle of Thudd's chest began to blink. *meep* . . . "Unkie Al!" said Thudd.

Thudd's purple button popped open and a purple beam zoomed out.

At the end of the beam was something furry. A flap of fur fell away.

Underneath was the familiar face of Uncle Al! He was Andrew and Judy's uncle, a top-secret scientist. He'd made Thudd and the Time-A-Tron.

"Hi, guys!" said Uncle Al. His teeth were chattering, but he was smiling.

"Uncle Al!" shouted Judy.

"Hiya, Unkie!" squeaked Thudd.

"Jumping gerbils!" said Andrew. "You really *are* in an ice age!"

"You've got that right, Andrew," said Uncle Al. "I'm still in Montana. But I'm located sometime between eleven thousand and twenty thousand years ago.

"But where are *you*?" asked Uncle Al. "Safe inside the cabin, I hope."

When Uncle Al contacted Andrew and

Judy by Hologram Helper, he could hear them, but he couldn't see them.

"Um, not exactly," said Andrew. "We're in the Time-A-Tron, floating in an ocean of boiling rock."

Uncle Al's frosty eyebrows went up. "Walt Disney on a walnut waffle!" he said. "What happened?"

"Thudd figured out that Doctor Kron-Tox kidnapped you and took you to an ice age," said Andrew. "We had to take the Time-A-Tron to rescue you."

Uncle Al shook his head. "It's great that you wanted to help me," he said. "But time travel is too dangerous. I'd rather be stuck in an ice age than put my favorite kids at risk."

"Uncle Al," said Judy. "The last purple-button message came from Doctor Kron-Tox."

Uncle Al frowned. "That doesn't surprise me," he said. "Kron-Tox grabbed one of my old Hologram Helpers."

bong . . . "Professor Dubble," said the Time-A-Tron. "There is trouble with the Fast-Forward button."

Uncle Al brushed off an icicle hanging from his nose. "Check the tachyon tubes and—"

gu . . . gu . . . guzzz

The Uncle Al hologram looked like it was dripping away. Uncle Al's voice was fading.

"Uncle Al!" yelled Judy. "You're disappearing!"

"It's the Hologram Helper batteries," said Uncle Al in a voice they could hardly hear. "They don't work well in the cold.

"Now I have something very important to tell you. Doctor Kron-Tox has hidden Professor Wilde . . ." *guzzzzzz* ". . . and he's planning to . . ." *guzzzzzz*

Before Uncle Al could finish his thought, his hologram completely dripped away!

KRUZZZAAAAAAH!

"He's gone!" cried Judy.

meep . . . "Look!" said Thudd, pointing to a bright dot streaking through the night sky.

Judy squinted to see it.

"A shooting star!" she said.

"We should make a wish," said Andrew.

bong . . . "We should wish to be somewhere else," said the Time-A-Tron. "That is no shooting star. That is the planet that will smash into Earth and create the moon!"

"Uh-oh," said Andrew.

"What can we do?" asked Judy.

bong . . . "Nothing," said the Time-A-Tron.

"Unless the Fast-Forward button begins to work very soon."

Judy grabbed her slipper and slammed the button.

Flack! Flack! Flack!

Nothing happened.

The sky was turning red. The tiny dot was growing into a globe of orange light.

Glowing chunks were falling away from it. Tails of fire streaked across the sky as it sped closer.

"What will happen to us?" asked Judy.

bong . . . "That depends on how strong Strongium is," said the Time-A-Tron.

Strongium was what the Time-A-Tron was made of.

meep . . . "Purple button blinking!" said Thudd.

Thudd's purple button popped open and a purple beam zoomed out. But there was no one at the end of it.

Tick . . . tock . . . tick . . . tock . . .

"It's Doctor Kron-Tox again!" said Judy.

A whispery voice began to speak:

My oh my oh my oh my!
What's that coming
from the sky?

Is it huge and dark
and lumpy?
Does it make you
awfully jumpy?

What will happen
when it crashes?
Will the Dubbles
turn to ashes?

What is to become of you?
What you don't know,
I surely do!

"HA! HA! HA!"
Tick . . . tock . . . tick . . . tock . . .
The fiery planet was so close that it filled the whole sky. The sea of molten rock churned and turned into waves.

bong . . . "Put in your earplugs, little Dubbles," said the Time-A-Tron.

Two pairs of earplugs dangled from a door in the control panel. Andrew and Judy stuck them in their ears.

Then Andrew squeezed his eyes shut and waited.

KRUZZZAAAAAAAAAH!

A humongous crash shook every bone in Andrew's body. His stomach fluttered up as the crash blasted them down and down.

When Andrew opened his eyes, flaming rock was zooming by the dome of the Time-A-Tron.

Andrew pulled out his earplugs. So did Judy.

"We must be miles deep inside the Earth!" said Judy.

Ahead of the Time-A-Tron was a glow as bright and yellow as the sun.

meep . . . "Core of Earth," said Thudd. "Like core of apple. Earth core is big lump of iron. Earth core hot, hot, hot! Seven thousand degrees! Surface of sun only five thousand degrees!"

bong . . . "Do not look, little Dubbles," said the Time-A-Tron. "The brightness will hurt your eyes."

Andrew and Judy turned away. It was getting awfully hot and sweaty inside the

Time-A-Tron. Judy fanned herself with her hand. Andrew wiped his face with his pajama sleeve.

bong . . . "We are almost past the core of the Earth now," said the Time-A-Tron. "We are slowing down."

"We're buried so deep," said Judy. "How are we going to get out of here?"

bong . . . "Ah," sighed the Time-A-Tron. "All we can do is follow the atoms of Montana. Perhaps the atoms will move up, but it could take millions of years."

Hooo . . . hooo . . . hooo . . .

Judy looked at Andrew. "What's that?" she asked.

"It's coming from below," said Andrew. "We'd better go down and see."

4 DON'T EAT THE PASSENGERS!

Hooo . . . hooo . . . hooo . . .

Andrew and Judy unbuckled their seat belts. Andrew pulled up the trapdoor in the floor. Then he and Judy climbed down the rope ladder to the lower compartment.

It was dark, but Andrew found the light switch and turned it on.

Hooo . . . hooo . . . hooo . . .

When Andrew turned toward the fuel tank, he was nose to beak with a small, feathery face. Its yellow eyes stared at him fiercely.

"An owl!" said Judy. "It's so tiny and cute! But how could it have gotten in here?"

meep . . . "Owl get into Unkie's lab," said Thudd. "Maybe follow prey animal into Time-A-Tron."

"A mouse or something?" Judy said.

chee chee chee

A chirpy sound was coming from a tangle of black tachyon tubes on the floor.

Andrew and Judy scrambled over to the tubes.

meep . . . "Look!" said Thudd.

Inside a broken black tube was a tiny, furry nose.

meep . . . "Shrew!" Thudd said.

Judy leaned down to see. The nose looked

like a mouse nose, but longer and pointier.

"Cheese Louise!" said Judy. "It's munching on a tachyon tube! That's why we're losing fuel!"

Judy glanced back at the owl. It hadn't moved, but it was staring at that twitching nose.

"Humph," said Judy. "I know owls eat things like mice and shrews. But there are only four creatures alive on Earth right now. Nobody is going to be eating anybody."

Andrew nodded. "We need to get the shrew out of the tube," he said. "Then we've got to fix the tube before we lose any more fuel."

Suddenly the pointy nose disappeared into the tube.

"Uh-oh," said Andrew.

He put his foot on the tube behind the shrew to keep it from moving back. Judy cupped her hands in front of the tube.

The shrew crept out, wobbled, and fell over into Judy's hands!

"Oh no!" said Judy. "I think it fainted! I'll take it upstairs."

While Judy climbed into the upper compartment, Andrew studied the hole in the tube. "Is there any tape around here?" he asked.

bong . . . "No, Master Andrew," said the Time-A-Tron. "Professor Dubble was kidnapped before he could stock the Time-A-Tron with tools and supplies."

Andrew scratched his head. Then he noticed something small and dark and round on the floor beneath the owl.

"I guess you can't expect owls to use litter boxes," Andrew said.

meep . . . "Not owl poop," said Thudd. "Owl pellet. Owl not got teeth. Owl eat whole animal. Owl stomach digest meat. Then stomach make bones and fur into lump called pellet. Owl throw up pellet, spit it out."

Andrew rolled the owl pellet along the floor with his slipper. It was hard and dry. He tapped it and it fell apart. Inside were little bones—and a tiny skull!

meep . . . "Mouse bones!" said Thudd.

Andrew examined the tachyon tube.

"Hmmmm," he murmured. "This tube is made out of soft stuff. I wonder . . ."

Andrew put one end of the broken tube inside the other. Then he pushed little bones through both parts to hold them together.

Andrew climbed the ladder up to the top compartment.

It felt cooler now. Outside, the melted rock had gone from yellow to reddish orange.

Judy's bathrobe was piled on the floor next to the chair. In the middle of the bathrobe was the shrew, curled into a ball.

"I think he's okay," said Judy. "He even ate some scraps from your stupid fudge."

"Super-duper pooper-scooper!" said Andrew. "And I fixed the broken tachyon tube!"

"Then let's try moving forward in time," said Judy.

Andrew and Judy fastened their seat belts. Then Judy smacked the Fast-Forward button.

Flack! Flack! Flack!

HNNNN . . . HNNNN . . . WOOHOOOO!

KNOCK, KNOCK. WHO'S THERE?

The display lit up.

4 BILLION YEARS AGO

Judy held down the Fast-Forward button.

bong . . . "Bravo, Miss Judy!" said the Time-A-Tron. "We are moving through time again!"

They had traveled 500 million years since they were trapped inside the baby Earth.

Andrew and Judy watched the gooey rock outside the Time-A-Tron change from fiery red-orange to dull brown.

meep . . . "Rock not so hot now," said Thudd.

bong . . . "Do check the Super-Peeper, little Dubbles," said the Time-A-Tron. "You can watch what is happening on the surface of the Earth."

The Super-Peeper showed a lumpy ball covered with pimples—and the pimples were steaming!

"Eeeuw!" said Judy. "The Earth looks *disgusting*!"

meep . . . "Earth got lotsa volcanoes now," said Thudd. "Volcanoes erupt! Throw up lotsa stuff from inside Earth. Lava. Gas. Steam.

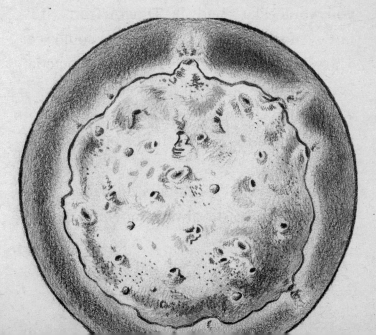

"Lava turn into land. Make little continents. Gas turn into air. Steam turn into
water!"

As Andrew and Judy watched, enormous
storms began to swirl over the Earth. Water
collected in the shallow places.

meep . . . "Rain make oceans," said Thudd.

bong . . . "And somewhere out there, life
is beginning," said the Time-A-Tron.

"Wowzers!" said Andrew. "It'll be great to
have company!"

bong . . . "It is not the kind of company
you would like," said the Time-A-Tron. "It is
not even the kind of company you could see.
The only things alive now are bacteria.
Perhaps you would call them germs."

Andrew and Judy watched as chunks of
land crept across the Earth like bugs across a
kitchen table.

meep . . . "Continents moving," said
Thudd. "Continents always moving. Crunch

together. Break up. Then smoosh together in different way. Move as fast as fingernails grow."

bong . . . "That is right, little friend," said the Time-A-Tron. "The changes you see inside the Super-Peeper take millions of years."

"Wowzers schnauzers!" said Andrew. "Our piece of land is creeping from the South Pole to the equator!"

600 MILLION YEARS AGO flashed the display.

chee chee chee

The shrew had scurried up the chair and skittered across Judy's hand.

"Ohhhh!" yelled Judy. Her hand flew off the Fast-Forward button.

BUH-BUH-BUH *ZNERKKK*!

The digital display stopped at 360 MILLION YEARS AGO.

KRAAAAAAAAACK! KRUUUUNK!

The Time-A-Tron dropped back into

normal time. Instantly, they were caught in a gushing river of rock. They were shooting up through the Earth like a cannonball!

SSSSSSSSSSSSS . . .

With a sizzle, the Time-A-Tron hit black water. An instant later, they burst to the surface. Through twisting pillars of smoke, Andrew saw blue!

"Wowzers schnauzers!" he yelled. "The sky!"

"Look!" said Judy, peering through the dome. "Land!"

A big wave rolled the Time-A-Tron sideways onto a patch of sandy beach. They were surrounded by ferns as tall as refrigerators. .

Beyond the beach was a forest of strange-looking trees. Their long, skinny trunks rose toward the sky. At the tops of the trees were bushy branches that looked like feather dusters.

Clack! Clack! Clack!

Andrew turned toward the sound. A fist was poking out of a fern and knocking on the Time-A-Tron's dome!

6 BEEPER

"What is *that*?" asked Judy.

bong . . . "It is *amazing*," said the Time-A-Tron. "Humans will not appear on Earth for more than three hundred million years!"

A face pushed its way through the ferns. The face had a big smile and lots of freckles and was surrounded by curly red hair.

"How did he get *here*?" asked Andrew, waving at the boy.

The boy motioned for them to come out.

"Let's go!" said Andrew.

bong . . . "It may not be safe out there," said the Time-A-Tron. "Tell the boy to come inside."

"Look!" said Judy. "He's sticking his tongue out at us!"

Andrew and Judy unbuckled their seat belts.

Judy looked around for the shrew. She saw a skinny little tail poking out of the compartment under the control panel. The shrew had found a place to hide.

"Okay, little guy," said Judy. "Stay put till we get back."

Andrew pulled open the door in the floor. Since the Time-A-Tron was on its side, Andrew and Judy slid into the lower compartment.

Andrew switched on the light. He looked for the owl, but it was nowhere to be seen.

bong . . .

The outer door opened.

Andrew poked his head outside. The air was hot and wet. Andrew breathed in the salty, fishy smell of the sea.

He hopped out and waved to the boy. "Hey there!" he said. "My name's Andrew."

"I'm Judy Dubble," said Judy, stepping through the door.

meep . . . "Thudd here!" squeaked Thudd from Andrew's pocket.

The boy came over to the door. He was wearing dirty green shorts and an orange T-shirt with a picture of a lizard on the front.

"Hi!" he said. "My name's Beeper. Beeper Jones. You're on *my* island!"

"How did *you* get here?" asked Andrew.

Beeper chuckled. "Doctor Kron-Tox dumped me here," he said.

"Why would Doctor Kron-Tox kidnap a bratty little kid?" asked Judy.

"He didn't kidnap me," said Beeper. "He's my uncle, but he makes me call him Doctor Kron-Tox. He said he dropped me off here to do stuff for him. But the real reason he dumped me is because I'm a pain.

"My uncle told me about you Dubble kids. He doesn't like you very much. Why are you in your pajamas?"

Judy put her hands on her hips and looked down at Beeper. "Because your stupid uncle kidnapped *our* uncle when we were getting ready for bed," she said crossly.

Beeper cocked his head and smiled. "Want to see some cool stuff?" he asked.

"Sure!" said Andrew.

"Andrew!" said Judy sharply. "We're not wandering off on some bizarre-o island. We could be eaten by a Tyrannosaurus or something."

Beeper laughed. "I *wish* there were dinosaurs here!" he said.

meep . . . "No dinosaurs for hundred million more years," said Thudd.

"Come on, Beeper," said Judy. "Get into the Time-A-Tron. We've got to rescue our uncle, then we'll get back to our own time."

"I can't leave without my stuff," said Beeper.

"What stuff?" asked Andrew.

"Stuff that I left in the forest," said Beeper. "I even have something that can help you find your uncle. But first, you need to help me carry my things."

Judy rolled her eyes. "I guess we have to," she said.

bong . . . "Do be extremely careful," said the Time-A-Tron. "Hurry back. And this is most important—do not go into the water."

"Why not?" asked Andrew.

bong . . . "Because I said so," said the

Time-A-Tron, with a bit of impatience.

"Okay," said Andrew. "We won't go swimming."

The beach was covered with large, cake-shaped rocks. Andrew stepped onto one of them . . . and slid off.

"Oofers!" he said. "These rocks are slippery!"

meep . . . "Rocks called stromatolites," said Thudd. "Made by special bacteria. Bacteria make mud stick together. Burp up lotsa oxygen, too. Baby Earth not got much oxygen till bacteria start burping three billion years ago!"

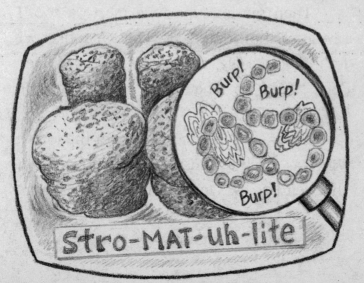

Stro-MAT-uh-lite

"Wowzers!" said Andrew, getting back on his feet. "Germs must have burped a lot in three billion years."

"Eeeeeuw!" said Judy, scrunching up her face. "I'm breathing *germ burps*!"

"That's so neat!" said Beeper, hopping from stromatolite to stromatolite across the beach.

Judy rolled her eyes. "So where did you get a name like Beeper?" she asked.

"'Beep' was the only word I said till I was four years old," said Beeper. "Everyone thought I couldn't talk.

"Then my grandpa took me to a zoo. I saw an octopus and a platypus! A zookeeper let me hold a big, fat, hairy tarantula spider. After that, no one could make me *stop* talking."

Beeper led them to the edge of the forest. Vines as thick as sausages hung down from the weird trees. On the ground, roots were tangled like fat snakes. The air smelled like a moldy cellar.

"What lives in the forest?" asked Andrew, wiping sweat from his forehead.

"Hoo boy!" said Beeper. "Wait till you see!"

7 BUG ZOO

Judy peered into the green gloom of the forest.

"There's no path," she said. "How do you know where you're going?"

"I make a trail by bending branches," said Beeper.

"Oh great," said Judy, rolling her eyes. "That'll be *real* easy to follow. Wait a minute."

Judy pushed her hands into her pajama pockets. She pulled out a pen, a dime, a tiny notebook, a spool of thread, and a bottle of glue.

Judy put back everything but the spool of

thread. She tied the loose end around a tree trunk. "We can follow this back," she said.

Beeper stuck out his tongue. "Let's go!" he said, leading the way through the tangle of trunks and vines and roots.

The ground was wet and slippery. Needles of sunlight poked through the umbrella of leaves high above. Water dripped from the treetops. They heard small splashes. Little scraping sounds came from inside rotting logs.

"I haven't seen a single bird," said Andrew. "Or even a squirrel."

meep . . . "No birds on Earth yet," said Thudd. "No squirrels. No mammals at all."

ffffff · · · *ffffff* · · ·

A shimmer of color flashed through a patch of sunlight. It was the transparent wing of a huge insect!

"Wowzers schnauzers!" said Andrew. "A dragonfly!"

"It's the size of a seagull!" said Judy.

"Isn't it *cool*?" said Beeper. "We're gonna take some back with us! My uncle's gonna have a theme park with prehistoric animals. I'm in charge of collecting insects and spiders and stuff."

"Um, the Time-A-Tron warned us not to fool around with things in the past," said Andrew.

"Yaaaaah!" cried Judy, doing a crazy dance. "A cockroach the size of a shoe just crawled over my foot!"

"I've got a bunch of those, too!" said Beeper. "I'll show you. We're almost there."

They came to a swampy place beside a pond. Giant dragonflies were gliding lazily over the dark water.

Hssssss . . .

A snakey sound came from under a fern. Something quick and brown—like a small crocodile—darted out. It snatched a dragonfly resting on a leaf and gobbled it down.

Beeper jumped over a log. "Here they are," he said.

Near the edge of the pond were wire cages. In one cage, two giant dragonflies fluttered their wings. In another cage, four cockroaches the size of footballs scuttled up the walls.

Behind these cages was a cage big enough for a large dog. Inside, a collie-sized scorpion was snapping its giant black claws. It reared its tail—with a sharp stinger at the end—up over its head!

"Don't worry," said Beeper. "She's just protecting her babies. See?"

As Andrew and Judy got closer, they saw that the scorpion's back was squirming with lots of white scorpions the size of kittens.

"Aren't they cute?" asked Beeper.

"Eeeeeuw!" said Judy. "They're *disgusting*!"

Beeper crouched next to a hollow log. "You've gotta see *this* guy!" he said.

The end of the log was covered with a screen. A scraping sound came from inside.

Andrew leaned over. "I can't see anything," he said. "It's too dark in there."

Andrew pulled his mini-flashlight out of a pocket, flicked it on, and looked inside.

ssssssssssssss . . .

8 GOOD-BYE!

The beam glinted off something shiny and brown.

Andrew made out a sandwich-sized head with long, twitchy antennas. Below them, sharp jaws opened like scissors. Lots of spiny legs stuck out from a long, armored body.

The beam of light made the creature zigzag quickly toward the back of the log.

"Yowzers!" said Andrew.

Beeper grinned. "It's a gigunda centipede," he said. "He's six feet long! Isn't he *beautiful*? Did you see those fangs? He's real venomous!

"But I don't have a cage for him. You've gotta help me carry this log back to your time machine."

"No way!" said Judy. "You can't just take these things back to our time! What if they got loose?"

meep . . . "Our time not good for them," said Thudd. "Food different. Air different. Future time got less oxygen."

Beeper looked at his collection of cages. "Gee," he said. "I don't want them to get sick or anything. But can't I take *something* back? How about a couple of cockroaches?"

"Oh great!" said Judy. "Wouldn't *those* be nice in the kitchen?"

Andrew smiled. "Remember when that

cockroach dragged us up through the kitchen drain?"

"What?" said Beeper.

"Puh-*leeeze*!" said Judy, kicking a tree. "I'm still trying to forget it. These cockroaches are so big, you could hitch them up like sled dogs!"

meep . . . "Mother cockroach lay fifty eggs every month," said Thudd. "In one year, mother cockroach and her babies make thirty thousand cockroaches."

Judy shuddered. "Beeper," she said, "it's you or your zoo. You can come with us or you can stay with them."

"Tum tee dum tee dum," muttered Beeper, walking up to the scorpion cage. "My uncle never told me how to take care of these guys. The scorpion looks kinda hungry."

Andrew nodded. "So let them go, and come with us."

Beeper tapped the centipede's log and

looked inside. "I guess it's good-bye, big guy," he said.

"Finally!" said Judy. "But before you let them out, give us a head start. I don't want to be around when you open those cages."

"Fraidy-cat!" chuckled Beeper, pulling up the latch on the scorpion's cage.

"Don't you dare!" said Judy.

"You're no fun," said Beeper. "But I'll count to twenty before I let them go."

"I'll stay with Beeper and help him," said Andrew.

"One . . . two . . . three . . . ," counted Beeper.

Judy clambered off through the muck.

By the time Beeper got to twenty, Judy was waving at them from a rock on the edge of the pond.

Andrew opened the dragonfly cage. In a moment, their rainbow wings were flitting above the pond.

Beeper opened the cockroach cage. The cockroaches didn't seem to know they were free.

"We'll have to pick them up and take them out," said Beeper. He reached in and grabbed the biggest one. Its legs scrambled madly in the air.

Andrew wrapped both hands around the next biggest one.

It felt like plastic. He put it down on the

mossy ground and it scuttled away.

The last two cockroaches skittered out on their own.

Beeper went to the scorpion cage.

"I'd better do this myself," said Beeper. "She trusts me."

Beeper lifted the door. "Good-bye, girl!" he said. "Good luck."

As the mother scorpion crawled away, two of the scorpion babies fell off her back. Andrew and Beeper gently picked them up and put them back on. The scorpion crept off into the forest.

Next, Beeper jumped on top of the giant centipede's log.

"Better get up here," said Beeper to Andrew. "I don't know what this guy will do."

Andrew hopped up behind Beeper. When Beeper pulled up the screen, the centipede waggled out—and started to creep onto the log!

Beeper reached behind him. There was a backpack on the ground. He grabbed it and shoved it between him and the centipede. The centipede skittered off in the opposite direction.

"Bye, guys!" shouted Beeper. "Maybe some of you will turn into fossils and I'll find you someday!"

Beeper hitched his backpack over his shoulder. He and Andrew sloshed along the muddy edge of the pond toward Judy.

"Come on," said Judy, hopping off her rock. "Let's get back to the Time-A-Tron before we run into more huge buggy things."

She led the way, following the thread.

"Anyone want a sandwich?" asked Beeper, reaching into his backpack.

"Sure," said Andrew.

"No thanks," said Judy.

Beeper threw Andrew a sandwich bag.

Andrew opened the bag and took a bite. "What is it?" he asked.

"Tuna and peanut butter," said Beeper. "My favorite."

"Interesting," said Andrew, taking another bite.

It wasn't long before they could see the green ocean between the tree trunks. Andrew spotted the eggy shape of the Time-A-Tron on the beach. The tide was higher now. Waves were splashing against it.

RUUUUUUUURRRRRR!

"Sounds like a train!" said Andrew.

"Sounds like thunder," said Judy.

The ground beneath their feet rolled like a wave.

meep . . . "Earthquake!" said Thudd.

Something strange was happening to the ocean—it was disappearing! It was getting sucked away from the shore. And it was carrying the Time-A-Tron with it!

THUDD

9 TSUNAMI!

"We can't let the Time-A-Tron get away!" yelled Andrew.

He shoved the half-eaten sandwich into his pocket and pushed through a tangle of vines.

"Noop! Noop! Noop!" said Thudd. "Gotta climb tree!"

"That's *nutso!*" said Judy. "We're losing the Time-A-Tron and you're telling us to go climb a *tree?*"

meep . . . "Tsunami coming!" said Thudd. "Giant wave made by earthquake! Tsunami wave can be hundred feet high!"

"Holy moly!" said Andrew.

Judy looked up. "Are these trees tall enough to keep us from getting washed away? Will the *trees* get washed away?"

"Just *climb!*" said Beeper.

He was already ten feet up a tree. It swayed as he climbed higher.

"Beeper's tree is too skinny for all of us," said Andrew. He found a fatter tree and started climbing.

"Hurry up," said Judy, following him.

The tree trunk was like the skin of a pineapple. The scaly bark kept snagging Andrew's pajamas. There were no branches to hang on to.

Andrew looked down. The beach and the ferns looked far away. Andrew felt dizzy.

meep . . . "Hurry!" squeaked Thudd. "Water coming!"

On the horizon, Andrew saw a thin, dark line. It was getting wider and nearer by the second.

Andrew and Judy were only halfway up the tree.

"Move it, Andrew!" yelled Judy.

"Wait a minute," said Andrew. "I've got to keep Thudd from getting wet."

The last time Thudd had gotten wet, his thought chips had gotten soggy. He had been in very bad shape.

Andrew hung on to the trunk with one hand and searched his pockets for a Bubble Bag. He'd invented the Bubble Bag to keep Thudd dry.

"Uh-oh," said Andrew. "I can't find my Bubble Bags. But I do have this."

He pulled out the bag with the half-eaten sandwich inside.

"Why are you stopping?" Beeper yelled from his tree.

"I'm going to use the sandwich bag to protect Thudd," said Andrew. "He can't get wet."

"Just don't dump my sandwich," said Beeper. "You can squeeze Thudd in on top of the bread."

"Okay," said Andrew.

Quickly, he stuffed Thudd in with the sandwich and tucked him back in his pocket.

Andrew and Judy scrambled up to the long, brushy branches at the top of the swaying tree.

The dark line on the horizon had become a huge wall of water rolling toward the shore. The nearer it got, the higher it got.

"The water is as high as the trees!" cried Judy.

"Hang on!" said Andrew.

KRAAAAAAAASHHH!

The water slammed into their tree. It was cold and hard. Andrew closed his eyes, held his breath, and clung tight to his branch. He felt the water dragging powerfully at the tree, bending it.

Suddenly the tree jerked loose! The wave swept them back into the forest. Andrew pushed his head between his arms to keep from being scratched by branches.

Then the wave began to go down and move in the opposite direction. It was dragging them back toward the beach.

Andrew lifted his head. Out of the corner of his eye, he caught a glimpse of orange. Beeper's T-shirt! Beeper was still up in his tree on the edge of the forest. He was pointing and yelling.

Andrew couldn't hear every word, but he thought he could make out "Time-A-Tron!"

THE BIG DUNK

Beeper scrambled down his tree and jumped into the water. He swam between floating trees to get to Andrew and Judy.

"We survived a giant tsunami!" shouted Beeper, climbing onto their tree trunk.

As the wave pulled away from the island, it left the beach covered with logs.

"We're getting hauled out to the deep sea!" said Judy.

The wave carried them so far out that the island looked like a distant dot.

Beeper pointed toward a tangle of tree trunks floating nearby. "I saw the Time-A-

Tron get dragged off with that pile of logs," he said.

"I don't see it," said Andrew.

"Maybe it sank," said Judy.

"We can dive to look for it," said Andrew.

"You remember what the Time-A-Tron said about the water?" asked Judy.

"It's a little late to worry about that," said Beeper. "But look what I've got!"

He unzipped his backpack and pulled out a small package of juice with a drinking straw attached. He yanked it off.

"You can use this to snorkel," said Beeper.

Beeper put one end of the straw in his mouth, bent the straw up, and dog-paddled with his face underwater.

Beeper lifted his head and smiled. "See?" he said. He reached into his backpack, pulled off two straws, and handed them to Andrew and Judy. "Breathe through your mouth," he said, "not your nose."

"I *know* how to snorkel," said Judy. "My parents taught me when I was three."

Andrew and Judy bent their straws, slipped off the tree trunk, and dipped their faces under the surface.

Rays of sunlight lit the green water.

On the sandy bottom, Andrew saw creatures that looked like they came from other worlds. Things that looked like giant ice cream cones with tentacles squirmed through the water. Huge bug-like animals crawled along the bottom. Fish with armored bodies swooped slowly over the sand.

Wowzers schnauzers! he thought. *I wish Thudd could tell me what these things are.*

But Thudd was tucked safely in his sandwich bag.

Andrew was happy to find something he recognized—colored branches of coral like the ones he'd seen when he'd been lost on the reef.

Something strange was moving behind a hill of coral. It looked like a giant snail shell. It was as big as a stove! Sticking out of the open end was a head that looked like a squid, but with dozens of wriggling tentacles.

Woofers! thought Andrew, swimming away. *Whatever that is, I hope it's not hungry.*

Andrew felt a poke. It was Thudd. Even though he was in a plastic bag with a sandwich, he'd managed to creep to the top of Andrew's pocket. Thudd was pointing.

At first, all Andrew could see was a big shadow. But then he glimpsed a silvery shine beneath the shadow—the Time-A-Tron!

Andrew began to swim toward the Time-A-Tron. Thudd poked him even harder.

Andrew lifted his head above the water, took the straw out of his mouth, and pulled Thudd out of his pocket.

Judy popped up beside Andrew and so did Beeper. Beeper blew water out of his nose.

"Thudd found the Time-A-Tron," said Andrew excitedly. "Let's go!"

"Noop! Noop! Noop!" said Thudd, his voice muffled inside the plastic sandwich bag. "Giant armored fish down there! Called Dunkleosteus. Big as bus! Look!" Thudd pointed to his face screen. It showed a frightful face. Instead of teeth, its jaws were filled with jagged saws.

"Dunkleosteus drag Time-A-Tron underwater!" Thudd continued. "Chew on Fast-Fins!"

"Uh-oh," said Andrew. "I guess *that's* why the Time-A-Tron didn't want us going into the water."

"How can we get the Dunkle-whatever away from the Time-A-Tron?" asked Judy.

"I want to see the Dunkleosteus!" said Beeper.

Judy rolled her eyes.

"Beeper," said Andrew, "do you have any more of those sandwiches?"

Beeper nodded. "I've got six left."

"Yes!" said Andrew. "We can use them to lure the Dunk away from the Time-A-Tron."

"I'll throw them," said Judy. "I'm the best pitcher in my softball league."

"Let's throw the whole backpack," said Andrew. "It will take the Dunk longer to get the sandwiches and give us more time to get to the Time-A-Tron."

"I hate to say it, Bug-Brain," said Judy. "But that's a good idea."

Beeper punched Andrew on the arm. "Will you get me a new backpack?" he asked. "I want one with lots of pockets."

"Sure!" Andrew smiled. "I've got an extra one at home."

Beeper pulled two small black cases out of his backpack and put them into his pockets. Then he pushed the backpack toward Judy.

"Here ya go!" he said.

Judy pulled herself up onto the tree trunk.

"Where's the Time-A-Tron?" she asked.

Andrew pointed.

Judy rolled the backpack into a tight ball and threw it far away from the Time-A-Tron.

Plash!

Andrew checked underwater to see what was happening with the giant fish.

The Dunkleosteus stopped chewing on the Time-A-Tron's Fast-Fins. It swam over to the backpack. It started to attack it!

The Time-A-Tron began to float slowly to the surface.

"Let's go!" yelled Andrew. "Before the Dunk finishes his lunch!"

They all swam as fast as they could between the logs and branches that cluttered the water.

Every time Andrew felt something go bump, he hoped it wasn't the Dunkleosteus.

In seconds, they reached the Time-A-Tron. It was floating on its side.

bong . . .

Its oval door slid open.

Andrew crawled in, then Judy. Beeper was pulling himself over the edge when . . .

"Yeeouch!" he yelped. "Something's got my pants!"

An ugly gray head rose up out of the water. It was as big as the front of a car.

"The Dunkleosteus!" yelled Andrew.

11 WHOSE HUMONGOUS TAIL IS *THAT*?

Judy stuck her head out the door. "Take off your pants!"

Beeper fished the two small black cases out of his pockets and tossed them through the door. Then he unbuttoned his shorts.

The monster fish head sank below the water—with Beeper's shorts between its snaggly jaws!

Beeper scrambled into the Time-A-Tron wearing just his lizard T-shirt and a pair of boxer shorts. His boxers had pictures of penguins on them.

Andrew slid the door shut.

bong . . . "Welcome back, little Dubbles,"

said the Time-A-Tron. "I was afraid I might not see you again. And who is our guest?"

"Beeper Jones," said Beeper. He bent down and picked up the black cases. "You're pretty cool for a time-travel machine! My uncle's time-travel machine just grunts."

"Beeper is Doctor Kron-Tox's nephew," said Andrew. "But he's a good kid."

bong . . . "Welcome, Master Beeper," said the Time-A-Tron. "Children, please prepare to leave immediately, before the Dunkleosteus returns to munch on the Fast-Fins. They have already been damaged.

"But I have good news. There is a bit more tachyon fuel than I thought. We may have enough to rescue your uncle and return to our own time."

"*May* have enough?" said Judy.

bong . . . "And only if we travel more slowly than we did before," said the Time-A-Tron.

"Let's go!" said Andrew, pulling down the

door that led to the top compartment.

Hooo . . . hooo . . .

The little owl was sitting on top of the tachyon fuel tank. It opened its beak and spread its wings.

"What a great little owl!" said Beeper.

He opened one of his small black cases, took out a gadget that looked like a remote control, and pointed it at the owl.

ping . . . ping . . . ping . . .

"It's a northern pygmy owl!" he said, reading a display at the top of the gadget.

"What have you got there?" asked Andrew.

"It's a DNA Detector," said Beeper.

meep . . . "All living things got DNA molecules," said Thudd softly from inside the sandwich bag. Andrew opened it.

"All DNA molecules different. Turtle DNA different from tiger DNA. Different kindsa owls got different DNA."

Beeper nodded. "My uncle gave me this thing so I could find creatures on the island. We can use it to find your uncle!"

bong . . . "Let us hope so," said the Time-A-Tron. "But for now, please do hurry. I shall make room for Master Beeper."

When they climbed to the upper compartment, a new silver-blue chair was rising from the floor behind Andrew and Judy's seat. Andrew, Judy, and Beeper strapped themselves in. Andrew took Thudd out of the sandwich bag and put him on the control panel.

Judy checked the compartment under the control panel. The shrew's beady brown eyes stared up at her. Its pointy nose twitched. Something stringy was hanging out of its mouth. It was eating the cords that held the earplugs!

Judy turned to Andrew and Beeper. "Is everyone ready?" she asked.

"Yup," said Andrew.

meep . . . "Okey-dokey," said Thudd.

"You bet!" said Beeper.

Judy held down the Fast-Forward button.

HNNNN . . . HNNNN . . . WOOHOOOOO!

The Fast-Fins began to spin. At first, the Time-A-Tron whirled sideways in the water. Then it rose straight up and fluttered just above the surface. As the Fast-Fins spun faster, balls of green light flickered around the Time-A-Tron.

BLAFOOOOOM!

"Nice ride!" said Beeper, leaning over the front seat. "What's that button you're pushing?"

"It's the Fast-Forward button," said Judy. "I have to hold it down till we get to twenty thousand years ago. That's when we start looking for Uncle Al."

"That's how *I* can help!" Beeper said. "I'll set the DNA Detector for human DNA."

The numbers on the digital display were flipping by more slowly than before:

246 MILLION YEARS AGO

185 MILLION YEARS AGO

93 MILLION YEARS AGO

Now and then, the sky was lit by an exploding star.

"Let go of the Fast-Forward button," yelled Beeper. "The DNA Detector says we're close to a human!"

bong . . . "I do not think so," said the Time-A-Tron. "We are approaching sixty-five million years ago. There are no humans here."

"It could be Professor Wilde!" said Andrew. "We've got to stop."

Professor Winka Wilde was one of Uncle Al's partners. She had been kidnapped before Uncle Al.

Judy let go of the Fast-Forward button.

BUH-BUH-BUH ZNERKKK!

The Time-A-Tron wobbled to a stop. They were in a dark green forest, next to a giant gray boulder.

Andrew rubbed his eyes. "Um, I thought I saw that boulder move," he said.

"Probably because the Time-A-Tron smacked into it when we landed," said Judy.

"Hoo boy!" said Beeper, peering down through the dome. "This boulder has a tail! A monster tail as thick as a tree trunk! And the Time-A-Tron is sitting on it!"

As Andrew looked around to see what the tail belonged to, his eyes met a pair of eyes.

Huge, dark, reptilian eyes were staring at him through the dome!

There's nothing on Earth like this, thought Andrew, *except a dinosaur!*

TO BE CONTINUED IN ANDREW, JUDY, AND THUDD'S
NEXT EXCITING ADVENTURE:

ANDREW LOST
WITH THE DINOSAURS!

In stores July 2005

TRUE STUFF

Thudd wanted to tell you more about baby Earth, but he was too busy keeping his friends safe from tsunamis and Dunkleosteuses. Here's what he wanted to say:

• For millions of years, Earth was a ball of molten rock because of all the asteroids and comets that kept crashing into it. But something else helped make the Earth hot and squishy.

The asteroids contained radioactive elements, like uranium. Over thousands of millions of years, radioactive elements change into other elements, like lead. As radioactive elements change, they give off heat.

The inside of the Earth is *still* hot and squishy because of radioactivity and the heat left over from those crashing asteroids!

• No one knows for sure where life began on Earth, but we do know that it had to be near water. When scientists search for life on Mars, they look for water. If there's water, there could be life!

• When the Earth was very young, there was almost no oxygen. The only creatures alive then were bacteria that lived without oxygen.

But then plant-like bacteria evolved. These creatures burped up oxygen—lots and lots of it—as plants do today. This oxygen actually poisoned the first creatures that lived on Earth! Most of them died. But some of them live today in places where there is little or no oxygen. Can you think of places where there is very little oxygen?

• Because they don't have lungs, insects

cannot suck air into their bodies like we can. Instead, air flows in through holes in their hard outer skeletons. But the air can't get very far inside, which keeps insects small.

Around 300 million years ago, some scorpions, centipedes, and insects grew to enormous sizes—much bigger than insects grow today. No one is sure how they grew so big. One idea is that there was more oxygen in the air, which made it easier for oxygen to get inside a larger creature.

• Insects and spiders were among the first creatures to live on land. Cockroaches were living on Earth at least 100 million years before dinosaurs arrived! Although lots of ants were stepped on by dinosaurs, ants are still here and dinosaurs aren't.

• Earthquakes release enormous amounts of energy. This energy travels in waves underground or through water. When it travels through water, it can create a tsunami.

Interestingly, a tsunami wave doesn't look different from a normal wave as it travels hundreds or thousands of miles through the ocean. You can't see the energy of the tsunami until it slams into the shore.

• Sometimes a tsunami is called a tidal wave. This name is not accurate, because tsunamis are not created by tides.

To learn about all the planets in our solar system and to see some great pictures, go to www.NASA.gov!

WHERE TO FIND
MORE TRUE STUFF

Want to find out more weird things about the universe, our solar system, and baby Earth? Read these books!

• *Universe* by Robin Kerrod (New York: DK Publishing, 2003). You'll see what's happening in our solar system and in galaxies trillions of miles away!

• *Born with a Bang: The Universe Tells Our Cosmic Story* by Jennifer Morgan (Nevada City, CA: Dawn Publications, 2002). In just a few pages—and lots of wonderful pictures—you'll find out what we know about where *everything* came from!

• *From Lava to Life: The Universe Tells Our Earth Story* by Jennifer Morgan (Nevada City, CA: Dawn Publications, 2003). The universe itself tells the story of how life on Earth began and of the enormous number of creatures—from bacteria to brontosaurs—that have lived here. It also tells about weird and amazing dangers—like huge asteroid crashes—that life has survived.

Turn the page
for a sneak peek at
Andrew, Judy, and Thudd's
next exciting adventure—

ANDREW LOST
WITH THE DINOSAURS!

Available July 2005

1 THIS IS BIG!

"Wowzers schnauzers!" shouted ten-year-old Andrew Dubble. Huge brown eyes were staring at him through the dome of his time machine, the Time-A-Tron. "I think it's a brontosaur!"

The Time-A-Tron had landed in a forest 65 million years ago. It had also landed on the long, thick, scaly tail of a humongous dinosaur!

The reptile eyes staring in at Andrew did not look pleased.

Judy, Andrew's thirteen-year-old cousin, leaned forward in her seat. "Cheese Louise!" she said. "Its neck is as long as a bus! It sure does look like a brontosaur."

"Naaaah," said Beeper Jones, the nine-year-old boy Andrew and Judy had found 300 million years ago. "That's no brontosaur."

Beeper pointed a gadget that looked like a remote control at the long-necked creature.

ping . . . ping . . . ping . . .

"The DNA Detector says it's an Alamosaurus," said Beeper.

meep . . . "Alamosaurus look like brontosaur," squeaked a voice from Andrew's pocket. It was Thudd, Andrew's little silver robot and best friend. "But brontosaurs not alive now. Brontosaurs already extinct."

Thudd pointed to a picture of the Alamosaurus on his face screen. "Alamosaurus long as two school buses. Weigh as much as forty cars."

The Alamosaurus opened its mouth. Inside were short, stumpy teeth.

"It looks angry," said Judy. "Angry enough to eat us!"

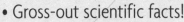

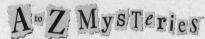
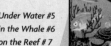